Playing by the Rules

A Story about Autism

Written by
Dena Fox Luchsinger

Illustrated by
Julie Olson

WOODBINE HOUSE 2007

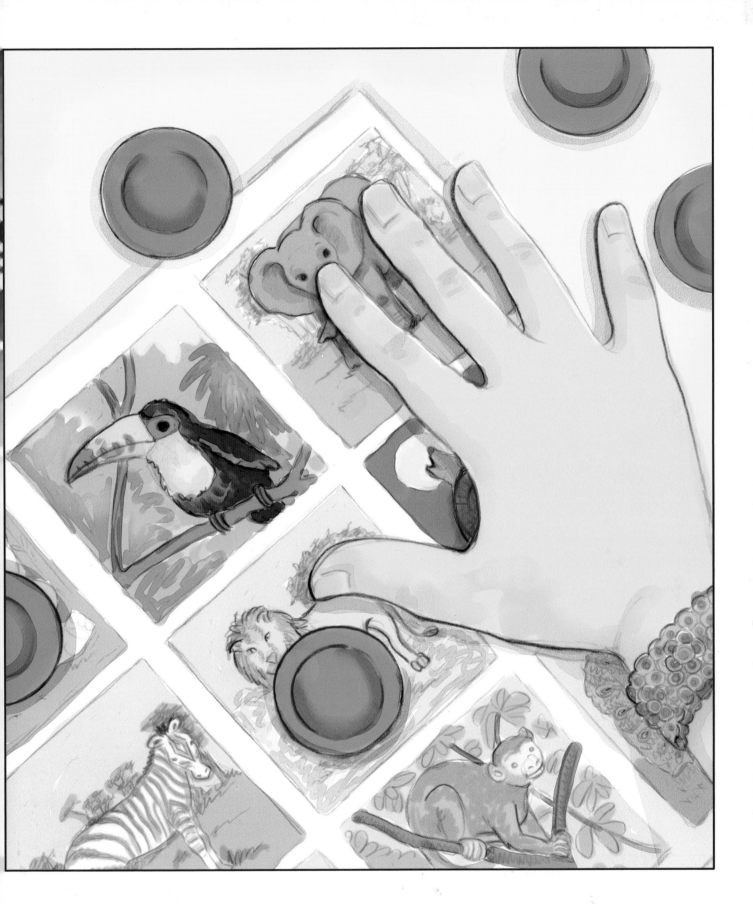

When the wolf howled I slapped a token down, but it didn't matter because Josh was faster.

"Sit down in your thinking chair and think, think, think!" said Josh. That's short for "Bingo." It's not really short because it takes longer to say, but Josh kind of has his own rules.

"You win," I grumped. "Again." Josh always wins at Animal Sounds Bingo because he knows exactly which animal is next on the CD.

Aunt Tilda plopped down next to Josh. "Can I play?" she asked.

Josh got up and left. He still wasn't too sure about Aunt Tilda. Great Aunt Tilda used to watch us when we were little, but then we moved away. This was her first visit in years, so she remembers us but we don't remember her.

Josh doesn't like new people for the same reason he doesn't like new shoes. They both rub him the wrong way. New people give Josh blisters in his head.

I pushed my bingo card to the side. "Let's play Cavityland!" I said. When I grow up, I'm going to be a dentist like my dad. When Josh grows up, he's going to be a sea lion. "Sounds fun, Jody," Aunt Tilda said to me. Then she turned around and asked Josh's back, "Where are you going, Josh?"

Josh kept walking, so I answered for him. "He only likes animal games," I said, digging out Cavityland. "But that's okay. It's more fun with two players."

In Cavityland, you have to get to the Tooth Fairy Palace with clean teeth to win. Josh came in right as I landed on Brilliant Brushing. "All right!" I said, skipping halfway to the end. Aunt Tilda was still way back on the Toothpick Trail.

Josh put a sentence strip in the middle of our game.
It had a drawing of a hand with the words "I want"
printed underneath. After that, Josh had put a little
picture of his *Babe* video on the Velcro. Josh doesn't
always communicate with pictures anymore, but he
has a hard time talking to new people. He wouldn't
even look at Aunt Tilda yet.

Aunt Tilda picked up the sentence strip and asked, "What's this?"

Josh put his head down and looked at the underneath part of his baseball cap.

"It's PECS," I said. "It's like talking with pictures. It says that Josh wants to watch *Babe.* I'll get Mom. HEY! MOOOOM!" I yelled in the direction I last saw Mom.

But Aunt Tilda shook her head. "No, Jody, don't bother your mother. I can get it. Where are the movies?"

I sighed. "In the hall closet."

"All right, honey. I'll be right back."

I leaned my head on my hand. Every time we play games around here, it's the same thing. There's always something to get for Josh, and it always takes ten hours to get it.

"Okay," Aunt Tilda said when she got back a minute later. "Whose turn is it?"

"Mine," I said grumpily. Then I noticed Aunt Tilda digging in her purse.

"What's that?" I asked.

"Caramel Goo-Pop. I brought it just for you."

I looked around. I didn't see Mom, and Dad wasn't home. Quickly, I ripped the wrapper off the sucker. And boy, was it gooey! It stuck to my teeth like bubble gum sticks to fur. Only don't ask me how I knew that. Anyhow, there was no way this yummy thing was going to end up on the cat—it was delicious! "Frank oo berry mush!" I drooled. Mittens looked at me suspiciously and left the room.

I grabbed the dice and rolled. Doubles! "I law a too! I law a too!" I yelled, still sucking goo. Losing Teeth is very good in this game.

Josh came in again and put another sentence strip down.

Aunt Tilda picked it up. "Should I get that?" It was a drawing of a cup.

I took the sucker out of my mouth. "Nah," I said. "Mom can get it." I turned to Josh. "Go get Mom, okay?" Josh left, which was good. I was winning.

Then Aunt Tilda tried to roll doubles to get rid of the Creepy Crusty Cotton Candy Coating that was decaying her teeth at a disturbing rate. If she got stuck now, I'd win for sure. "No doubles! No doubles!" I told the dice as she rolled. "No!"

She got doubles and moved ahead. Then I noticed Josh was back, still holding the PEC and chewing on his sleeve. "Hey, MOM!" I bellowed. I wondered where she was.

"In the bathroom!" came the muffled reply.

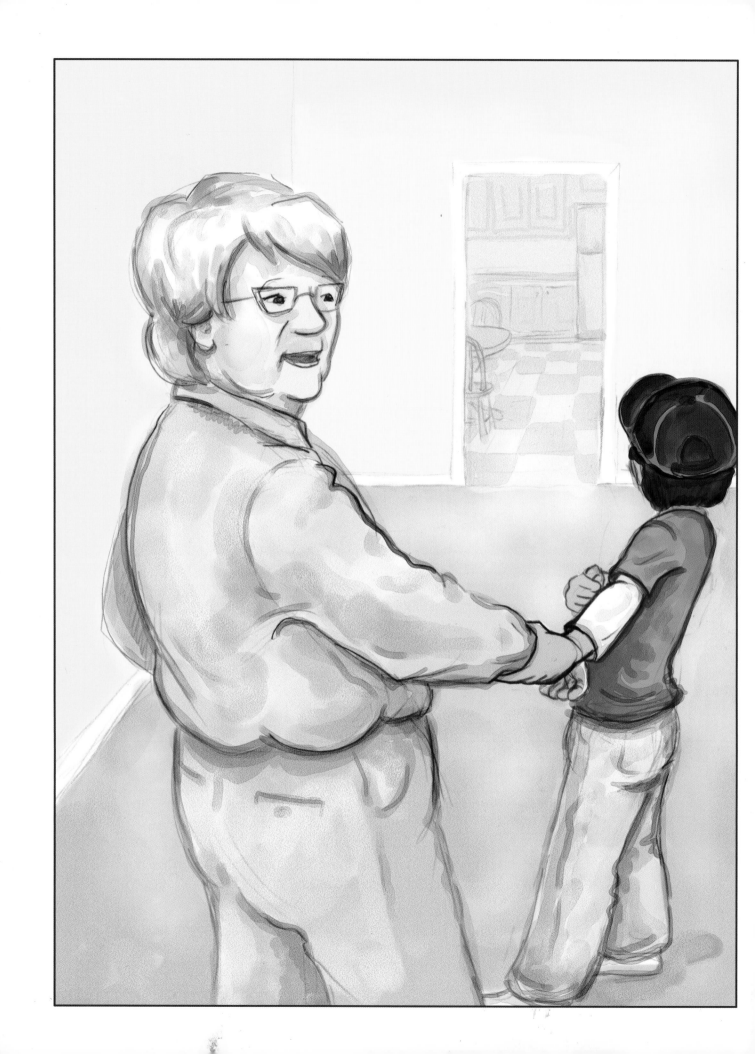

Aunt Tilda took the sentence strip. "I'll get him a drink. What does he like?"

"Anything—but don't give him Hyper-2000 soda. We're only allowed to have it on special occasions." I grabbed the dice.

Josh took Aunt Tilda's hand and pulled it in the general direction of the fridge without actually looking at her. "I want soda, please," he said. He was warming up to her. I was impressed.

"I'll be right back," she said.

"No rush," I said sadly. I'd just gotten stuck in the Gooey Gunk Glob. I tapped my fingers on the board. Aunt Tilda was telling Josh why he couldn't have soda. It was taking a while, so I saved us both some time and rolled until I got out of the Glob. Then I went to see what was keeping Aunt Tilda.

"He only wants soda!" Aunt Tilda said. "What should I do?"
"I want soda, please," Josh repeated, trying to get around Aunt Tilda to the
fridge. "Just say no," I said. "Give him juice. He likes juice, too."

Aunt Tilda looked a little nervous. "Uh, no soda, Josh. Juice." She showed
Josh the juice carton and looked to me for support. I nodded impatiently.
Can't anyone figure out Josh without me? Aunt Tilda poured Josh a cup of
juice. "Here you go," she said. Josh took the juice and wandered off.

I handed Aunt Tilda the dice. "Go," I said.

A minute later, Josh went back into the kitchen. "Is he okay?" Aunt Tilda asked. "Oh, shoot." Now she landed in the Gunk Glob.

Josh came over and shoved a soda can at me. I cracked the top and gave it back without thinking. I was winning, and Aunt Tilda was stuck in muck. I crossed my fingers and rolled.

"That's it," said Aunt Tilda graciously. "You win."

"Woo hoo! I win!" I screamed and tossed my sucker in the air. Then I did my special winner dance. "I win, I am the win-nah! Winner, winner boo-gay! A-woogy, woogy woo-gay!"

Josh covered his ears and left the room. He doesn't like loud, annoying sounds. Then Aunt Tilda kind of yelled, "I'm going to go see what Josh's up to," so I guess she didn't, either. My dad says I'm a Bad Winner and I like winning too much. But isn't winning like the whole point? I threw in a moon walk.

Only, doing the Winner Boogy by yourself isn't as much fun, so after a minute I stopped and followed Aunt Tilda and Josh.

Josh was in the family room playing with his collection of realistic-looking animal guys. He likes to line them up, and his favorites are sea mammals and wild cats. Some people don't think there's an order to animals like there is to the ABCs and numbers, but they're wrong. Whenever Josh gets a new animal, he always knows exactly where it goes.

I got there just in time. "Aunt Tilda, no!" I yelled. Aunt Tilda was reaching out for a cheetah. From the way she was smiling, I don't think she was trying to be mean.

Aunt Tilda didn't understand. She picked up some animals. "Look, Simba, it's Mr. Manatee," she said in a funny voice. Josh screamed. When his animals get messed up, it ruins his whole life until they're put back.

"Put them back, Aunt Tilda! Put them back!" I yelled. Aunt Tilda looked startled, but she put them down. "Now back away from the animals, lady," I told her. "Nice and slow."

Josh quickly rearranged his guys and calmed down. I know how he feels because I like to keep my crayons in rainbow order and I hate it when they get messed up. But it's even harder on Josh.

"What did I do?" Aunt Tilda asked.

"Nothing," I told her. "It's okay. You just don't know the rules to Josh's game yet."

Aunt Tilda looked confused.

"I know," I said. "Let's play Life!" More attention to me and less to Josh—for now—would solve everything.

"Okay," she said uncertainly. "Do you think Josh wants to play?"

"Nah," I said. "Actually, Josh is pretty good at Life. It's just that he plays by his own rules. See?"

Aunt Tilda looked at Josh, who was now perfectly happy adjusting the manatee ever so slightly. He took a sip of Hyper-2000 from his can. "I guess I can understand that . . . ."

"Oh, and can I have a soda?" I asked. "I mean, Josh got one . . . ."

"Um . . . ."

And that's how I beat Aunt Tilda TWO games in a ROW! And also why Josh and I got to stay up and JUMP on the SOFA way past BEDTIME!! Only that's NOT allowed!!! But JUST this time it's OKAY!!!! And Mom got the GOO off the CAT with a scissors!!!!! And I hope Aunt Tilda can STAY for a YEAR!!!!!! 'Cause I LIKE her!!!!!!! And MITTENS likes her!!!!!!!!

And I think JOSH LIKES HER, too!!!!!!!!!

THE END

About the Author

Dena Fox Luchsinger is the author of *Sometimes Smart is Good / A Veces es Bueno Ser Inteligente* (Eerdman's, 2007) and founder of Proyecto Down, a non-profit program serving families of children with Down syndrome in Monterrey, Mexico. After living and traveling extensively in Central and South America, she currently lives in Wasilla, Alaska, with her husband and three children, one of whom has the dual diagnosis of Down syndrome and autism.

About the Illustrator

Julie Olson grew up with six brothers and two sisters in southern Indiana. She found her own way among her siblings by moving out west and becoming an artist. Her passions are raising her three children and illustrating children's books, including *Already Asleep* (Keene Publishing, 2006).